Written by Moira Butterfield
Illustrated by Simon Mendez

PRODUCED FOR CHAD VALLEY TOYS
489-499 Avebury Boulevard,
Central Milton Keynes, MK9 2NW

www.argos.co.uk

ISBN 978-1-4454-3169-7
Batch Code: S22716
Made in Guangzhou, China

Muddypaws

It was a special day for Ben. He had a new puppy!
"I'll teach you all the things I know," said Ben.
"But first I need to choose a name for you. I'll need
to think hard about it. It has to be just perfect."

"I don't really mind what name you choose,
as long as you give me lots of cuddles," thought
the new puppy.

Ben looked around his bedroom to see if he could find an idea for the perfect puppy name.

"I'll look in my storybook," he said, but none of the names in the book were right for his new puppy.

"I think I'll leave you to hunt for names," thought the new puppy. "I'd rather look behind that flowerpot."

The little puppy crept over...

He sniffed...

...and then
he climbed.

He didn't mean to knock the flowerpot over, but...

Oops!

That's just what he did.

He made muddy pawprints everywhere.

"Let's go to the park. I might be able to think of a good name there," said Ben.

"I'd rather look behind that tree," thought the little puppy.

So he ran...

...and he ran.

He didn't mean to jump
in the mud, but...

squelch!

That's just what he did.

He made muddy pawprints everywhere.

Ben's neighbours were having a party in their garden. "One of the guests might be able to think of a good name for you," said Ben. "Let's go and ask them."

"I'd rather look in the pond," thought
the new puppy.

So he leaned over...

...and he leaned over a little bit more.

He didn't mean to fall in the pond,
but...

Splosh!

That's just what he did.

He made muddy pawprints everywhere.

"We'd better go home and clean you up," said Ben.
"I'd rather go digging in the garden," thought
the new puppy.

So he dug...

...and he dug...

...and he dug.

This time he found
lots of things...

...a lost ring...

...an old spanner...

...and a toy car that Ben had lost.

He didn't mean to bring all
that mud indoors, but...

Pitter Patter!

... that's just what he did.

He made muddy pawprints everywhere.

And he didn't mean to find a name for himself at last, but... guess what? That's *just* what he did!

"You are the muckiest, muddiest, funniest puppy there ever was. There's only one name for you," laughed Ben.

"Muddypaws!"